PENELOPE FINKLE:

PASSION IN LONDON

BY:ALLY_BAKER

Printed in USA

Published by : Ally_Baker

Cover Image: Produced by: Ally_Baker

© Copyright 2016

ISBN-:13: 978-1533188045
ISBN-10: 1533188041

All Rights Reserved

No part of this publication may be reproduced or transmitted in any form whatsoever, electronic, or mechanical, including photocopying, recording, or by any informational storage or retrieval system without express written, dated and signed permission from the author.

By reading this you accept these terms and conditions.

Table of Contents:

Chapter One "The Story Begins".. - 5 -

Chapter Two "To Luton, We Go"... - 17 -

Chapter Three "A Tale Told".. - 27 -

Chapter Four "The Photograph".. - 35 -

Chapter Five "An Untraveled Road".................................... - 43 -

About the Author:

Ally Baker is a multi-talented "Mystery and Thriller" author who has been churning out exciting tales packed full of intrigue and suspense for over twenty years. Born on the sunny beaches of Southern California, Ally moved to the picturesque shores of New England after earning an Undergraduate Degree in Literature from Columbia University.

    The history and lore that have woven themselves into the Eastern Seaboard have inspired many
of the American Literary greats. Like legend Stephan King, Ally draws upon her community and the culture it is built upon to create enthralling works of suspense that are grounded in reality.

Chapter One

"The Story Begins"

I CAN STILL REMEMBER THE DETAILS LIKE I KNOW MY OWN ADDRESS. IT WAS APRIL OF 1958 – WE HAD JUST HAD A LONG WINTER AND THE DAYS WERE FINALLY STARTING TO WARM UP. FAMILIES OF JAYS AND BLACKBIRDS FREQUENTED THE PARKS AND FLOWERS AND BLOSSOMS WERE BLOOMING IN FULL, PAINTING A BEAUTIFUL PICTURE ACROSS LONDON.

I WAS GOING TO VISIT A DEAR FRIEND OF MINE, MISS PENELOPE FINKLE – OR PENNY, AS I CALLED HER. SHE WAS A CLEVER WOMAN – ALWAYS HAD A MIND FOR WORKING THINGS OUT AND OVERLOOKING THE OBVIOUS TO FIND THE HIDDEN SECRET IN ANYTHING THAT SHE CAME ACROSS. I SUPPOSE THAT'S WHAT MADE HER SUCH A GOOD PRIVATE INVESTIGATOR. ALTHOUGH NONE OF THE POLICEMEN WOULD ADMIT IT, NO ONE IN THE WHOLE OF THE COUNTRYSIDE COULD NAVIGATE A TRICKY PUZZLE BETTER THAN PENNY COULD. LONDON HAD BEEN QUIET FOR WINTER – IT WAS MUCH TOO COLD AND MISERABLE TO DO ANYTHING. AS SUCH, THERE WAS NOT MUCH BUSINESS FOR PENNY. BUT SPRING BROUGHT WITH IT JOY AND HAPPINESS AND, THIS YEAR, THE FILMING CREW FOR A NEW MOVIE, *PASSION IN LONDON*. EVEN IF BUSINESS WAS SLOW FOR PENNY, SHE WOULDN'T RESIST THE URGE TO HAVE A LOOK AT THE SET.

I FINALLY REACHED HER HOUSE AND, AFTER SHOOING HER NEIGHBOR'S CAT, KNOCKED THREE TIMES ON HER BIG HARDWOOD DOOR. I HEARD FOOTSTEPS APPROACHING FROM BEHIND THE DOOR, A pause, then three distinct noises – a chain drop, a bolt slide and a key turn – before the door creaked open.

"Andrea, my dear friend," she said, taking my coat and hanging it on a hook. "I wasn't expecting you so soon!"

"This is the time we agreed upon, my friend," I reminded her. "Tuesday morning for morning tea."

"Is that today?" she said. "My, I lost track of time! My sister has had their fifth child, you know. A beautiful baby boy born two days ago. I've been caught up in my sewing."

I passed my congratulations on through her and she showed me her new sewing projects – a patchwork blanket and a small pile of little outfits for her new nephew.

"Have you been outside today?" I asked her. She shook her head. "Spring has finally come!" I continued. "And I've heard that they have started filming *Passion in London* now."

Penny's eyes lit up at the mention of filming. "Oh, I would very much like to have a sticky-beak through the set," she said. "We shall go after we have had tea!"

I took my place on the armchair near the coffee table and waited while Penny went to make a pot of tea, scoping the room around me. The winter drapes were heavy and dark across the windows, still closed, though letting a thin slit of sunlight drift in through the crack between them. A small lamp stood near Penny's sewing machine, providing just enough light for her sewing. The fireplace homed smoldering red embers that were evidently a beautiful display of dancing flames just the

NIGHT BEFORE. ON THE MANTELPIECE WAS A ROW OF PICTURE

FRAMES AND PORTRAITS OF HER LATE HUSBAND-TO-BE WHO WAS CALLED TO FIGHT IN WORLD WAR II SHORTLY AFTER HE PROPOSED. UNLIKE MANY OTHERS, THEY OPTED TO WAIT UNTIL HE RETURNED BEFORE MARRYING. HE NEVER CAME BACK FROM THE WAR. SINCE THEN, PENNY HAS REFUSED ANY MAN WHO SHOWED INTEREST IN HER. ALBERT WAS HER FIRST AND ONLY LOVE AND SHE FELT AS THOUGH SHE WOULD BE BETRAYING HIM AND THE DREAMS THAT THEY HAD TOGETHER. SHE WAS LOYAL, AND SHE CAME OUT STRONGER BECAUSE OF IT.

AFTER A MOMENT OR TWO, THERE WAS AN URGENT KNOCK AT THE DOOR AND PENNY RUSHED OVER TO IT, MUMBLING SOMETHING ABOUT UNEXPECTED VISITORS AND FORGETTING TO LOCK THE DOOR AFTER LETTING ME IN. WHEN SHE HAD OPENED THE DOOR, I COULD HEAR A MAN'S VOICE THAT SOUNDED RUSHED AND URGENT.

"WELL, YOU HAD BETTER COME IN THEN," SAID PENNY.

THE RESONATING SOUND OF THREE SETS OF FOOTSTEPS VIBRATED THROUGH THE CREAKY FLOORBOARDS AS PENNY CAME INTO THE FAMILY ROOM WITH TWO MEN FOLLOWING BEHIND HER. ONE OF THE MEN APPEARED TO BE IN HIS SIXTIES, HIS GRAY HAIR WAS STARTING TO BALD ON TOP AND HIS BELLY LOOKED LIKE HE WAS SMUGGLING HALF-A-MELON UNDER HIS SHIRT. BROAD-FRAMED SPECTACLES WERE PERCHED ON HIS NOSE AND HIS MUSTACHE TWITCHED WITH EVERY BREATH. I HAD NO HESITATION IN RECOGNIZING HIM AS DETECTIVE GEORGE WORTHINGTON.

THE OTHER MAN – WHOM I DID NOT RECOGNIZE – LOOKED TO BE IN HIS EARLY TWENTIES. HE WAS A HANDSOME FELLOW WITH DARK BROWN HAIR, BLUE

EYES, AND HIS FACE WAS CLEANLY SHAVEN. HE WAS DRESSED NEATLY IN A LAUNDERED POLICE UNIFORM AND WAS MUCH THINNER THAN THE DETECTIVE. HE SEEMED TO HAVE THE STRONG YOUTH AND VIGOR OF A MAN FRESH TO THE JOB. DETECTIVE WORTHINGTON INTRODUCED THE YOUNG MAN AS SERGEANT ROBERT COLLINS WHO HAD RECENTLY TRANSFERRED FROM WINCHESTER TO THE LONDON POLICE FORCE.

"MISS FINKLE, I UNDERSTAND THAT YOU MUST BE INCREDIBLY BUSY NOW THAT WINTER HAS FINALLY PASSED," THE DETECTIVE SAID. "BUT WE HAVE A SERIOUS MATTER OF UTMOST URGENCY THAT NEEDS TO BE TENDED TO AND, ALTHOUGH SERGEANT COLLINS MAY NOT AGREE WITH ME, WE NEED YOUR HELP."

I LOOKED AT THE YOUNG MAN AGAIN, HIS CHEEKS NOW BLUSHING FROM THE DETECTIVE'S STATEMENT AND HIS EYES SCANNING THE ROOM AROUND HIM.

"WHY DON'T YOU AGREE WITH THE GOOD DETECTIVE?" I ASKED HIM. EVERYONE KNEW THAT PENNY WAS THE BEST THERE WAS, BUT WHY WOULD HE THINK OTHERWISE?

"HE STILL THINKS THAT WOMEN SHOULDN'T BE INVOLVED IN SUCH MATTERS," THE DETECTIVE ANSWERED.

"BEG YOUR PARDON, SIR, BUT I UNDERSTOOD THAT THAT CONVERSATION WAS CONFIDENTIAL," SAID SERGEANT COLLINS, HIS FACE NOW RED AS AN OVERRIPE TOMATO.

MY EYES TRAVELED QUICKLY TO PENNY – SHE NEVER MUCH LIKED THAT MANY MEN STILL THOUGHT THAT SHE WOULDN'T BE ABLE TO DO THE JOB RIGHT BECAUSE SHE WAS A WOMAN. SHE HAD ALREADY GAINED THE DETECTIVE'S RESPECT ON MANY OCCASIONS, BUT STILL OFTEN FOUND HERSELF IN THIS SITUATION. HER EYES GLEAMED WITH THE

CHALLENGE.

"MR COLLINS," SHE BEGAN, STARING AT THE YOUNG MAN.

"SERGEANT COLLINS, MA'AM," HE CORRECTED.

PENNY'S SMILE DANCED ACROSS HER FACE.

"THOUGH I DON'T NEED TO PROVE MYSELF TO YOU," SHE CONTINUED. "I WOULD HAVE YOU KNOW THAT I HAVE BEEN DOING THIS SINCE BEFORE YOU WERE BORN. I WORKED IN THE POLICE FORCE DURING WORLD WAR II WHEN ALL OF THE ABLE MEN WERE FIGHTING, AND MOVED ON TO WORKING AS A PRIVATE INVESTIGATOR. THE KIND DETECTIVE HERE KNOWS ME ALL TOO WELL, SINCE WE HAVE WORKED TOGETHER FOR THE LAST TWENTY YEARS OR SO. IT'S NOT GOOD TO UNDERESTIMATE A WOMAN, SERGEANT, AS THAT WOMAN MAY VERY WELL BE MUCH BETTER AT

CERTAIN THINGS THAN YOU."

SERGEANT COLLINS LOOKED TAKEN ABACK AND SEEMINGLY HAD THE TEMPERAMENT OF A LITTLE BOY BEING LECTURED BY HIS MOTHER. AVOIDING HER GAZE, HE LOOKED OVER AT ME.

"AND DON'T YOU WORRY ABOUT MISS WRIGHT EITHER," PENNY SAID. "SHE KEEPS ME COMPANY WHILE I WORK – MY ASSISTANT, I SUPPOSE YOU WOULD SAY. NOW, WON'T YOU BOTH SIT DOWN AND HAVE TEA WITH US?"

"MISS FINKLE, WE MUST CONTINUE WITH WHAT BUSINESS WE HAVE COME FOR," THE DETECTIVE SAID.

PENNY RAISED HER EYEBROW AT THE DETECTIVE AND REACHED HER ARM OUT TOWARDS THE LOUNGE SEAT IN A WELCOMING MANNER.

"DETECTIVE, HOW DO YOU EXPECT ME TO HELP YOU WITHOUT MY CUP OF TEA?" SHE INSISTED.

THE DETECTIVE SMILED AT PENNY AND RAISED A HAND TO SILENCE SERGEANT COLLINS FROM SAYING ANYTHING.

"VERY WELL," HE SAID. "WE SHALL HAVE TEA WITH

YOU."

Penny's eyes shone as she went to the kitchen to resume preparing the tea. When she returned with a tray that balanced a large white and blue teapot, four matching gold-trimmed teacups, a milk jug, a sugar dish and a small plate of shortbread biscuits, the detective and Sergeant Collins had settled themselves onto the lounge. She served the tea to her guests and positioned herself in her favorite armchair.

"Now," she said, taking a sip of her tea. "What matter is so urgent that it just can't wait?"

"A kidnapping," Sergeant Collins blurted.

"Miss Finkle," the detective continued. "I'm sure you are aware that there is a movie being filmed in London – *Passion in London*?"

Penny nodded for him to go on.

"Well, the starring actress, Miss Eileen Garner, has mysteriously gone missing and we suspect that she has been kidnapped."

"Oh dear," she said. "Why would someone want to kidnap her?"

"We don't know – that's why we're here," Sergeant Collins said.

"They had just finished setting up and were due to start today," the detective said. "Everyone was ready for filming, though, no one could get in contact with Miss Garner. She was not in her trailer, her bed looked like it had not been slept in and there was nothing to indicate a struggle. Everything looked as it should–"

"Except that Miss Garner had disappeared," Penny finished.

"Precisely," said the detective.

Penny had another sip from her teacup and

sat thoughtfully for a moment. I could almost see the cogs turning inside her head and wondered what she was thinking. Where was she going to start with this one? At last, she rested the teacup and saucer on the arm of her chair and straightened herself.

"Where was Miss Garner last seen?" Penny asked.

"Reports say that she was last seen rehearsing in her trailer," the detective said. "Though, the cleaner says that the trailer looked as if it hadn't been used since she cleaned it yesterday. She was the one who raised the alarm. She said that no one had seen Miss Garner since noon yesterday."

"I see," Penny sighed. "So, we have nothing?"

"We have something more," Sergeant Collins said.

"Continue," Penny urged.

"Well," he started. "Miss Garner has an understudy who claims to be quite close to her. When asked if she had seen her, the understudy said that one of the cameramen, Mr Ernest Snieder, seemed to have an interest in Miss Garner and she saw them arguing two nights ago – that was the last time she saw Miss Garner. At this stage, he's our prime suspect."

"And where is he now?" she said

"We don't know," said the detective.

"So, Mr Snieder is also missing?" she asked.

"Correct," said Sergeant Collins.

"How very interesting," Penny said. She slumped back into her armchair, eyes closed and rubbed her thumb and forefinger over her forehead. After a moment or two, she finally spoke again.

"Her understudy – what was her name?" she

SAID.

"MISS HENRIETTA BROWNLEY, MA'AM," SERGEANT COLLINS SAID.

"YES, I SHALL SEE HER NOW," PENNY DOWNED THE REMAINDER OF HER TEA, ROSE TO HER FEET AND LOOKED AT THE DETECTIVE. "WILL YOU TAKE US THERE?"

"MA'AM, DON'T YOU WISH TO FIND MR SNIEDER, FIRST?" SERGEANT COLLINS ASKED, PUZZLED.

"DO YOU QUESTION MY ABILITY, SERGEANT?" PENNY RAISED AN EYEBROW.

"NO, MA'AM," HE SAID. "I JUST THOUGHT THAT YOU WOULD BE MORE CONCERNED WITH FINDING THE PRIME SUSPECT THAN WASTING TIME TALKING TO SOMEONE WHO HAS ALREADY GIVEN A STATEMENT."

"ARE WE ON A DEADLINE?" PENNY ASKED.

"ONLY IF WE WANT HER TO STAR IN THE MOVIE," THE DETECTIVE SAID. "IN WHICH CASE, WE HAVE ROUGHLY TWENTY-FOUR HOURS OR THEY WILL START FILMING WITHOUT HER."

"HOW IMPORTANT IS THIS MOVIE, EXACTLY?" SHE ASKED.

"IT'S DEEMED TO BE BIG, MA'AM," SERGEANT COLLINS SAID. "THEY PREDICT IT WILL BE VERY PROFITABLE – BUT ONLY IF MISS GARNER IS STARRING. IF WORD GOT TO THE PUBLIC THAT SHE'S MISSING, EVERYONE WILL BE DEVASTATED AND NO ONE WILL SEE THE FILM."

"THEN WE SHALL FIND HER BEFORE WORD GETS OUT," PENNY SAID. "AND TO DO THAT, I NEED TO SEE MISS BROWNLEY."

I HELPED PENNY GATHER UP THE DISHES AND TOOK THEM TO THE KITCHEN WITH HER, LEAVING DETECTIVE WORTHINGTON AND SERGEANT COLLINS IN THE FAMILY ROOM FOR A MOMENT. I COULD SEE WHY SERGEANT COLLINS WAS CONFUSED BY HER WANTING TO SEE MISS BROWNLEY – IT WAS, INDEED, LOOKING BAD FOR ERNEST SNIEDER AND MISS BROWNLEY HAD

ALREADY GIVEN A STATEMENT. IN A TONE LOW ENOUGH SO THAT THE MEN WOULDN'T HEAR US, I ASKED HER WHY MISS BROWNLEY WAS HER FIRST POINT OF CALL.

"THAT'S A SECRET, MY DEAR," SHE WHISPERED, WINKING AT ME AND PLACING HER FOREFINGER OVER HER LIPS. "I WISH TO GET HER AUTOGRAPH."

I HAD KNOWN PENNY FOR A VERY LONG TIME AND I HAVE NEVER ONCE DOUBTED HER ABILITY TO SOLVE A MYSTERY. BUT I MUST ADMIT, THIS REQUEST DID SEEM QUITE PECULIAR. WE GATHERED OUR BAGS AND COATS AND REUNITED WITH DETECTIVE WORTHINGTON AND SERGEANT COLLINS OUTSIDE, PENNY ENSURING THAT HER DOOR WAS SUFFICIENTLY LOCKED. WE CLIMBED INTO THE DETECTIVE'S ASTON MARTIN AND HEADED TOWARDS THE SET OF *PASSION IN LONDON*. IT TOOK ROUGHLY HALF-AN-HOUR TO DRIVE THERE, IN WHICH PENNY NEVER LOOKED AWAY FROM THE WINDOW.

"HOW CURIOUS…YES, CURIOUS, INDEED," SHE MUMBLED ONCE OR TWICE, BUT WAS OTHERWISE SILENT.

WHEN WE ARRIVED AT THE SET, WE WERE GREETED BY THE DIRECTOR OF THE FILMING – MARTIN J. POSTLETHWAITE. PENNY TOOK THE OPPORTUNITY TO ASK HIM WHAT HE KNEW OF THE KIDNAPPING.

"ONE DAY SHE WAS HERE, THE NEXT SHE WASN'T," HE SAID. "IT'S CAUSED A GREAT INCONVENIENCE, REALLY. WE'RE ON A TIGHT SCHEDULE FOR FILMING, YOU KNOW. WE NEEDED TO START THIS MORNING TO BE ON SCHEDULE. NOW THE FILMING WILL BE RUSHED – AND WITH ONE CAMERAMAN SHORT, TOO."

"MR POSTLETHWAITE, WHAT DO YOU MEAN BY BEING ONE CAMERAMAN SHORT?" PENNY ASKED HIM.

"ONE OF OUR CAMERAMEN WAS HARASSING MISS GARNER," HE SAID. "I CONFRONTED HIM ABOUT IT TO ENSURE A SMOOTH FILMING. HE DIDN'T SEEM TO LIKE THAT AND THREATENED TO LEAVE. I DIDN'T THINK HE would – he's paid well – but I knew I shouldn't have trusted him."

"Ernest Snieder," Penny said.

"Yes," he replied.

"How was he harassing Miss Garner?" she inquired.

"Miss Garner said that he was filming her and photographing her outside of the scheduled filming time," he said. "She also said that he made some remarks that she deemed inappropriate – it was quite concerning really. Her understudy supported her claim, adding that he was spotted outside Miss Garner's trailer while they were rehearsing."

Penny thanked Mr Postlethwaite for his assistance and asked where Miss Brownley could be found. He directed us over to the set where she was expected to be rehearsing. She was exactly where he thought she would be and was looking quite frantic with the filming crew bustling around her, changing the scene.

"Miss Brownley, may I have a word with you, please?" Penny began.

"It must be quick," she replied, flicking through the rehearsal papers that she held in her hands. "I'm very busy today with Miss Garner being missing. I was very close with her, I do hope she's alright."

"Miss Brownley, you're her understudy, correct?" she asked.

"That's right," Miss Brownley said. "We often rehearsed together and were both excited to be working on this film together."

"I see," Penny thought for a moment. "But if you're her understudy, then you're not actually being filmed with her, are you?"

"Am I being interrogated?" Miss Brownley said. "I cared about Miss Garner – we were

FRIENDS. UNDERSTUDIES DO NOT APPEAR ON FILM UNLESS THEIR ACTOR OR ACTRESS IN UNABLE TO FULFILL THEIR ROLE. BUT EVEN SO, WE ARE THEIR MORAL SUPPORT AND THEIR BIGGEST FRIENDS. WE WOULDN'T WISH ANYTHING BAD TO HAPPEN TO THEM. NOW, IF YOU WILL EXCUSE ME, I HAVE WORK TO DO."

"ONE LAST THING, MISS BROWNLEY," PENNY STOPPED MISS BROWNLEY FOR A MOMENT. "CAN I HAVE YOUR AUTOGRAPH, PLEASE? IT'S FOR MY NIECE – SHE'S A BIG FAN OF YOURS."

MISS BROWNLEY PAUSED FOR A MOMENT AND LOOKED AT THE PEN AND PAPER THAT PENNY HELD OUT TO HER. SHE GLANCED BACK TO THE FILMING CREW, AND QUICKLY SCRIBBLED SOMETHING ON THE PAPER – PENNY THANKING HER – BEFORE RUSHING AWAY. I READ THE NOTE WITH PENNY. IT SAID, *KEEP MOVING FORWARD*, FOLLOWED BY HER SIGNATURE. WITH A SMILE ON HER FACE, PENNY CAREFULLY FOLDED THE NOTE AND TUCKED IT INTO HER PURSE FOR SAFE-KEEPING.

WE RETURNED TO WHERE DETECTIVE WORTHINGTON AND SERGEANT COLLINS WERE STANDING AND PENNY ASKED IF WE COULD SEE MISS GARNER'S TRAILER. AFTER SEEKING PERMISSION FROM MR POSTLETHWAITE, WE PROCEEDED TO WHERE THE TRAILERS WERE GATHERED. WHEN WE REACHED MISS GARNER'S TRAILER, I ENTERED THROUGH THE DOOR WITH DETECTIVE WORTHINGTON AND SERGEANT COLLINS AND SEARCHED THE TRAILER FOR ANY CLUES. WE HAD ALREADY SEARCHED FOR A FEW MINUTES BEFORE REALIZING THAT PENNY WASN'T IN THE TRAILER WITH US. I SUGGESTED THAT PERHAPS SHE WAS SEARCHING OUTSIDE, BUT WHEN I LEFT THE TRAILER, SHE WAS A FEW TRAILERS OVER TALKING TO A MAN WHO APPEARED TO BE ONLY NINETEEN OR TWENTY. BY THE TIME I REACHED THE TWO OF THEM, THE CONVERSATION HAD ENDED AND PENNY WAS THANKING HIM FOR HIS ASSISTANCE. I ASKED HER

WHAT ASSISTANCE HE PROVIDED, BUT SHE ONLY SMILED AT ME WHILE WE WALKED BACK TO THE TRAILER. WE THOROUGHLY SEARCHED THROUGH THE TRAILER ONCE MORE, BUT STILL CAME UP EMPTY. THERE WAS NO CLUE IN THE TRAILER WHATSOEVER AND DETECTIVE WORTHINGTON AND SERGEANT COLLINS WERE BEGINNING TO FEEL FRUSTRATED.

"WE'RE NOT GETTING ANYWHERE HERE," SERGEANT COLLINS SAID, THROWING HIS HANDS IN THE AIR. "WE'RE JUST GOING AROUND IN CIRCLES."

"DETECTIVE," PENNY SAID. "DIDN'T YOU SAY THAT THE CLEANER WAS THE ONE WHO DISCOVERED THAT MISS GARNER WAS MISSING?"

DETECTIVE WORTHINGTON NODDED AT PENNY AND SAID THAT THE CLEANER HAD ALREADY FINISHED HER ROUNDS AND HAD GONE HOME FOR THE DAY. WE HUNTED DOWN HER ADDRESS AND BEGAN TO HEAD OVER TO HER PLACE TO ASK HER SOME QUESTIONS.

Chapter Two
"To Luton, We Go"

THE JOURNEY TOOK US WEST FOR ABOUT AN HOUR BEFORE WE FINALLY CAME TO THE STREET WHERE SHE LIVED. IT WAS DOWN A DARK ALLEYWAY – WE HAD TO PARK AT THE END AND WALK DOWN TO HER HOME. THERE WAS A FOUL ODOR FILLING THE AIR AND THE STREET WAS FULL OF GARBAGE. THE RESIDENTS OF THE STREET WERE LOOKING OUT OF THEIR DOORS AND WINDOWS, OBSERVING OUR EVERY MOVE. FOR A CLEANER WHO WORKS FOR SUCH WELL-TO-DO PEOPLE, I EXPECTED THAT SHE WOULD LIVE IN A MUCH NICER PLACE – OR AT LEAST MORE HYGIENIC. DETECTIVE WORTHINGTON EXPLAINED THAT THIS SEEMED TO BE MORE COMMON THAN YOU WOULD THINK. I PITIED THE WOMAN AND WONDERED WHAT SHE HAD GONE THROUGH TO BE FORCED TO LIVE HERE. WE FINALLY CAME TO HER DOOR WHERE SHE WAS ALREADY STANDING, ALERTED BY HER NEIGHBORS OF THE STRANGERS IN THE STREET. HER FACE WAS FILLED WITH SURPRISE WHEN WE STOPPED IN FRONT OF HER.
"MRS HODGKINS?" PENNY SAID.
"DEPENDS ON WHO'S ASKING," SHE REPLIED, LOOKING BEHIND US AT HER GATHERING NEIGHBORS.
"MA'AM, WE'RE LOOKING FOR MISS GARNER," SERGEANT COLLINS SAID, RECEIVING A SCOWL FROM THE DETECTIVE.
"WELL, YOU AIN'T GONNA FIND HER 'ERE," SHE SAID LOUDLY, RESTING HER HANDS ON HER HIPS.
"MRS HODGKINS, DO YOU MIND IF WE ASK YOU SOME QUESTIONS?" PENNY ASKED QUIETLY. "IT WOULD HELP DEARLY WITH OUR INVESTIGATION."
WE STOOD IN SILENCE FOR A MOMENT, WAITING FOR MRS HODGKINS TO ANSWER. HER EYES TRAVELED ACROSS EACH OF US AND BACK TO HER NEIGHBORS

BEFORE SHE LET HER ARMS FALL TO HER SIDE. SHE LET OUT A SIGH AND STEPPED TO THE SIDE OF HER DOOR.
"YOU HAD BETTER COME IN, THEN," SHE SAID.
PENNY THANKED HER FOR HER COMPLIANCE AND LED THE WAY INTO THE HOUSE. IT TOOK A WHILE FOR MY EYES TO ADJUST. THERE WAS VERY LITTLE SUN SHINING THROUGH THE SINGLE, SMALL WINDOW AND WHAT LITTLE LIGHTING THERE WAS SEEMED TO BE VERY DULL. THE AIR WAS THICK AND MUSTY, AND EVERYTHING AROUND US FELT DAMP. WHEN MY EYES FINALLY ADJUSTED, I SAW A SMALL TABLE IN THE CORNER AND A LARGE MATTRESS HIDDEN BEHIND A DELICATE CURTAIN. CONSIDERING THE STATE THAT THE BUILDING ITSELF WAS IN – LET ALONE, THE WHOLE STREET – MRS HODGKINS HAD MADE THE MOST OF HER HOME. THE SMALL KITCHEN SEEMED TO BE AS CLEAN AS IT COULD POSSIBLY GET AND THE ROOM LOOKED TO BE MOSTLY ORGANIZED. IN THE MIDDLE OF THE TABLE WAS A VASE FILLED WITH A BUNCH OF DRIED LAVENDER THAT LET OFF A COMFORTING SCENT – ENOUGH TO GENTLY MASK THE FOUL ODOR THAT DRIFTED IN FROM OUTSIDE. OUT OF THE CORNER OF MY EYE, I SAW THE CURTAIN MOVE SLIGHTLY AND THREE PAIRS OF CURIOUS EYES SCOPING OUT THEIR VISITORS FROM BEHIND THEM – MRS HODGKINS' CHILDREN, I ASSUMED. I SMILED AND WAVED AT THE CHILDREN, RECEIVING THREE LITTLE WAVES IN RETURN.
"MRS HODKINS," PENNY BEGAN.
"PLEASE, CALL ME SANDRA," MRS HODGKINS INTERJECTED.
"I UNDERSTAND THAT YOU WERE THE ONE TO NOTICE THAT MISS GARNER HAD NOT BEEN IN HER TRAILER?" PENNY CONTINUED.
"THAT'S RIGHT," SHE SAID. "THE BED WAS STILL MADE FROM WHEN I TURNED IT DOWN THE PREVIOUS AFTERNOON. I TURN IT DOWN EARLIER THAN EVERYONE ELSE'S BECAUSE I KNOW THAT SHE LIKES

TO LAY DOWN STRAIGHT AFTER WORKING ON THE SET. THAT'S WHY I THOUGHT IT WAS ODD WHEN I WENT TO CLEAN HER ROOM THIS MORNING. HER TRAILER IS THE FIRST PLACE SHE GOES AFTER WORK."

"WHAT TIME DOES SHE USUALLY FINISH WORK?" PENNY ASKED.

"AROUND FIVE IN THE AFTERNOON, MA'AM," SHE SAID.

"AND WHAT TIME WERE YOU THERE?" THE DETECTIVE ADDED.

"I USUALLY TRY TO GET THERE AT FOUR, BUT I WAS RUNNING LATE YESTERDAY. MY LITTLE ONE IS NOT FEELING VERY WELL, YOU SEE," MRS HODGKINS NODDED TOWARDS THE CURIOUS EYES STILL PEERING AROUND THE CURTAIN. "I COULDN'T GET THERE 'TILL HALF-PAST. USUALLY, MISS GARNER'S TRAILER IS MESSY AND NEEDS A LOT OF CLEANING. BUT NOT LAST NIGHT – THERE WASN'T MUCH TO DO AT ALL. I WAS SO RELIEVED THAT I DIDN'T THINK MUCH OF IT REALLY."

"CAN YOU TELL ME WHAT YOU DID CLEAN UP LAST NIGHT, SANDRA?" PENNY SAID.

MRS HODGKINS NODDED AND THOUGHT FOR A MOMENT.

"THERE WASN'T MUCH," SHE SAID. "THERE WAS A GLASS THAT I PUT AWAY. IT WAS NEAR HER SINK – THOUGH IT HAD BEEN CLEANED, WHICH WAS ODD. MISS GARNER NEVER WASHES HER DISHES, LET ALONE PUTS THEM NEAR THE SINK. USUALLY, THE SINK IS THE CLEANEST PART IN HER TRAILER."

MRS HODGKINS LET OUT A LAUGH AT HER OWN AMUSEMENT. IF THE REASON FOR OUR VISIT HAD BEEN DIFFERENT, I WAS SURE THAT WE WOULD HAVE ALL FOUND THAT STATEMENT AMUSING.

"THERE WAS SOMETHING ELSE, THOUGH," SHE SAID.

PENNY URGED HER TO CONTINUE.

"I REMEMBER CHECKING HER TRASH," SHE SAID. "THERE WAS ONLY SOME SCRUNCHED UP PAPER IN IT –

JUST A FEW SMALL PIECES – SO, I PICKED OUT THE PAPER AND DIDN'T WORRY ABOUT CHANGING THE BAG."

"DO YOU STILL HAVE THOSE PAPERS?" PENNY ASKED.

"I MAY HAVE," SHE SAID, RISING TO HER FEET AND HEADING TO A MAKESHIFT WARDROBE.

MRS HODGKINS RUSTLED THROUGH THE CLOTHES, FINALLY PULLING OUT A NEAT, BLACK COAT THAT SEEMED HER SIZE. SHE DELVED HER HANDS INTO EACH OF THE POCKETS BEFORE FINALLY PULLING OUT A SMALL HANDFUL OF SCRUNCHED UP PAPERS AND HANDED THEM TO PENNY. PENNY OPENED UP THE NOTES AND STARTED SCANNING WHAT THEY READ. I GLANCED OVER TO SEE WHAT THEY WERE. ONE APPEARED TO BE AN OPENED ENVELOPE WITH MISS GARNER'S POSTAL ADDRESS ON IT AND A RETURN ADDRESS THAT I DID NOT HAVE A CHANCE TO READ. THE OTHER WAS A HANDWRITTEN NOTE THAT SEEMED TO HAVE COME IN THE ENVELOPE.

"HAVE YOU READ THESE?" PENNY ASKED.

MRS HODGKINS SHOOK HER HEAD. I ASSUMED THAT SHE HAD INTENDED TO THROW OUT THE NOTES BUT HAD FORGOTTEN ALL ABOUT THEM. I WATCHED AS PENNY FLATTENED THE NOTES THEN FOLDED THEM CAREFULLY, PUTTING THEM IN HER PURSE. SHE THANKED MRS HODGKINS FOR HER HELP AND WE WENT ON OUR WAY.

I WAS THE FIRST TO CLIMB BACK INTO THE CAR, FOLLOWED BY SERGEANT COLLINS. BEFORE DETECTIVE WORTHINGTON AND PENNY ENTERED THE CAR, I SAW HER SAY SOMETHING TO HIM AND SHOW HIM SOMETHING IN A SMALL BOOK THAT I DID NOT RECOGNIZE. I WONDERED WHAT IT WAS AND WHAT SHE SAID, THOUGH I DID NOT ASK HER.

THE NEXT LEG OF OUR JOURNEY TOOK US NORTH-EAST FOR ROUGHLY TWO HOURS. ONCE AGAIN, SHE WAS SILENT FOR THE DURATION OF THE CAR TRIP

WITH THE EXCEPTION OF AN OCCASIONAL CHUCKLE. I DIDN'T WANT TO INTERRUPT HER TRAIN OF THOUGHT, THOUGH I DID WONDER IF SHE HAD ANY IDEA OF WHERE MISS GARNER MIGHT BE AND WHO THE KIDNAPPER WAS. WE WATCHED THE SUN SET AS WE TRAVELED AND, BEFORE TOO LONG, WERE SURROUNDED BY THE INTENSE DARKNESS OF A STARLESS NIGHT. WE BEGAN TO FEEL AS THOUGH WE WERE ALONE – ONLY SEEING TWO OTHER TRAVELING CARS ON OUR JOURNEY. TIRED-EYED AND WEARY, WE SOON ENTERED THE TOWN OF LUTON. AFTER A FEW MINUTES, WE FINALLY CAME TO A SMALL HOTEL THAT APPEARED TO HAVE A RESTAURANT ATTACHED TO IT.

"WE WILL STAY HERE TONIGHT," PENNY SAID.

DETECTIVE WORTHINGTON AND SERGEANT COLLINS BOTH LOOKED AT EACH OTHER AND SHOOK THEIR HEADS. HAD WE COME ALL THIS WAY JUST TO STAY THE NIGHT? I THOUGHT THAT WE WOULD HAVE RETURNED TO LONDON TO SLEEP. SERGEANT COLLINS OBVIOUSLY FELT THE SAME, ASKING PENNY THE VERY SAME QUESTION THAT I WAS THINKING.

"I HEAR THE FOOD IS NICE HERE," WAS ALL THAT SHE SAID.

IT SEEMED THAT EACH OF US HAD RESIGNED TO THE FACT THAT WE WOULD BE STAYING TO BOTH EAT AND SLEEP TONIGHT. WHETHER OR NOT PENNY HAD A REASON FOR COMING HERE, I COULD NOT TELL. BUT I DID KNOW THAT OUR TIME WAS RUNNING OUT IF WE WISHED FOR MISS GARNER TO STAR IN HER FILM. AS WE WALKED THROUGH THE BIG ENTRANCEWAY OF THE HOTEL, I WAS AMAZED BY WHAT I SAW. I HAD NEVER STAYED IN SUCH AN EXTRAVAGANT PLACE BEFORE. THE STAIRWELL WAS LARGE AND SPECTACULAR, THE BIG CENTRAL CHANDELIER GLISTENED WITH THE LIGHT BOUNCING OFF THE GLASS SPEARS THAT DANGLED AT ALL DIFFERENT LENGTHS. THERE WERE POTS OF EXOTIC AND COLORFUL PLANTS SEATED EITHER SIDE OF THE

RECEPTION DESK AND LINING THE STAIRWELL. THE RESTAURANT WAS TO THE LEFT OF THE HOTEL RECEPTION, EACH TABLE ORNAMENTED WITH A CANDLE AND FRESH BOUQUET OF ROSES.

WE WERE SOON BOOKED IN FOR THE NIGHT AND ESCORTED TO OUR ROOMS BY THE CONCIERGE. THE ROOMS OCCUPIED A NEAT DOUBLE-SIZED BED, A LARGE DESK AND ARMCHAIR, A SMALL LOUNGE SEAT AND A PLATTER OF DRINKS. A BROAD DOOR LED TO A LARGE BATHROOM CONTAINING A TOILET AND JACUZZI TUB. I OPENED THE HEAVY CURTAINS TO FIND A GLASS DOUBLE-DOOR THAT OPENED ONTO A BALCONY WHERE TWO CANE CHAIRS AND A MATCHING TABLE COULD BE FOUND. I FRESHENED UP AND WENT TO THE RESTAURANT TO HAVE DINNER WITH MY COMPANIONS. FOR DINNER, I ENJOYED A DELICIOUS PLATE OF LAMB ROAST AND VEGETABLES ACCOMPANIED WITH A HEARTY RED WINE. CONVERSATION WAS SUPERFICIAL AS DETECTIVE WORTHINGTON AND SERGEANT COLLINS WERE ONLY FOCUSED ON THE KIDNAPPING AT HAND. IT SEEMED AS THOUGH THEY WANTED PENNY TO SPILL THE BEANS ON WHAT SHE THOUGHT ABOUT THE CASE, BUT PENNY DIDN'T BUDGE.

"I JUST DON'T SEE THE POINT IN TALKING ABOUT COMPLETELY UNRELATED TOPICS WHEN MISS GARNER'S LIFE COULD BE IN DANGER!" SERGEANT COLLINS INTERJECTED, THROWING HIS HANDS IN THE AIR.

"*MR COLLINS*," PENNY SAID, SHAKING HER HEAD. "YOU DON'T WANT TO WEAR OUT THIS TIRED BRAIN, DO YOU?"

"HOW MANY TIMES MUST I TELL YOU? IT'S *SERGEANT* COLLINS!" SERGEANT COLLINS POUNDED HIS FISTS ON THE TABLE.

"YOUNG MAN," PENNY RAISED HER FINGER TO SERGEANT COLLINS. "WHEN YOU START ACTING LESS LIKE A CHILD AND MORE LIKE A SERGEANT, THEN –

AND ONLY THEN – WILL I CALL YOU *SERGEANT COLLINS*."

"I THINK THAT IS ENOUGH FOR TONIGHT," DETECTIVE WORTHINGTON DOWNED HIS DRINK AND ROSE TO HIS FEET. "IF YOU WILL EXCUSE ME, I THINK THAT I WILL RETIRE FOR THE NIGHT. SERGEANT COLLINS," HE DIRECTED HIS GAZE TO THE FURIOUS MAN BESIDE HIM. "YOU SHOULD DO THE SAME."

WE SAID OUR GOODNIGHT'S TO THE TWO MEN AND WATCHED AS THEY LEFT THE RESTAURANT TO GO TO THEIR ROOMS. SERGEANT COLLINS APPEARED TO BE VENTING HIS FRUSTRATIONS TO DETECTIVE WORTHINGTON AS THEY DUCKED OUT OF OUR SIGHT. I STARED AT MY DEAR FRIEND WHO HAD NOW SWAPPED HER EMPTY GLASS OF WINE FOR A POT OF TEA. I WONDERED WHY SHE REFUSED TO CALL SERGEANT COLLINS BY HIS TITLE. SURE ENOUGH, HE SEEMINGLY QUESTIONED HER EVERY MOVE IN A CHILDISH MANNER, BUT THAT DIDN'T STOP ME FROM THINKING THAT SHE WAS, PERHAPS, A LITTLE TOO HARSH ON HIM.

I DIDN'T KNOW HOW MUCH PENNY KNEW ABOUT MISS GARNER'S KIDNAPPING, NOR DID I WANT TO QUESTION HER AS SERGEANT COLLINS DID. AS FAR AS I WAS CONCERNED, MY HEAD WAS SPINNING WITH THE POOL OF APPARENTLY USELESS INFORMATION THAT WE RECEIVED TODAY. IT SEEMED AS THOUGH WE WERE NO CLOSER TO FINDING OUT WHERE MISS GARNER MIGHT BE OR WHO COULD POSSIBLY BE INVOLVED WITH HER ABSENCE. USUALLY, I WOULD DEFEND PENNY'S INTEGRITY, KNOWING THAT, SURELY, THIS TRIP MADE SENSE TO HER – THAT ANOTHER CLUE WAS TO BE FOUND. THOUGH, SHE DID NOT QUESTION ANYONE, NOR DID SHE SEEM TO BE LOOKING FOR ANYTHING. SHE JUST LOOKED AS THOUGH SHE WAS ENJOYING A NICE HOLIDAY.

PENNY POURED THE TEA AND I STAYED TO HAVE SOME WITH HER. OUR CONVERSATION WAS MORE

INTERESTING THAN WHEN THE MEN WERE AT THE TABLE WITH US. SHE SEEMED TO BE MORE RELAXED AND RELIEVED THAT SHE WOULDN'T BE RECEIVING AN INTERROGATION FROM SERGEANT COLLINS.

"I THOUGHT THEY WOULD NEVER LEAVE," SHE SAID TO ME WITH A SMILE ON HER FACE.

"YOU DIDN'T WANT THEM HERE?" I QUESTIONED. PERHAPS THAT WAS WHY SHE SPOKE TO SERGEANT COLLINS LIKE THAT.

"WHO WANTS TO ENJOY AN EVENING WITH WORK ACQUAINTANCES?" SHE LAUGHED, SLUMPING BACK INTO HER CHAIR. "I MUCH PREFER TO ENJOY IT WITH A FRIEND. AFTER ALL, WE HAVE MUCH TO CATCH UP ON."

I FELT TOUCHED BY HER SENTIMENT AND RELIEVED THAT HER CONVERSATION WITH SERGEANT COLLINS WAS NOT ENTIRELY AS IT SEEMED – RATHER, THAT IT WAS ALL IN PENNY'S PLAN TO ENJOY AN EVENING NOT DISCUSSING BUSINESS. TIME PASSED QUICKLY AS WE CAUGHT UP ON ALL THAT WE HAD MISSED OVER THE WINTER. BY THE TIME WE HAD FINISHED OUR THIRD POT OF TEA, THE STAFF WERE TIDYING UP AROUND US AND THE KITCHEN HAD WELL AND TRULY CLOSED. PENNY HAD NOT DISCLOSED ANYTHING TO ME ABOUT THE KIDNAPPING

THROUGHOUT THE NIGHT, THOUGH THAT DIDN'T MEAN THAT SHE DID OR DID NOT HAVE ANYTHING ON IT. MY EYES WERE DROOPING AND MY BODY FELT HEAVY. I EXCUSED MYSELF FROM OUR CONVERSATION AND SAID GOODNIGHT TO MY DEAR FRIEND.

"WON'T YOU ALSO BE RETIRING FOR THE NIGHT?" I SAID TO HER.

"I'LL HAVE JUST ONE MORE POT OF TEA," SHE SAID AND BID ME GOODNIGHT.

I LEFT THE RESTAURANT, LINGERING AT THE DOORWAY JUST LONG ENOUGH TO OBSERVE PENNY FOR A MOMENT. IN HER MOMENT OF SILENCE, SHE RECLINED BACK IN HER CHAIR AND RUBBED HER BROW WITH HER THUMB AND FOREFINGER. SHE SHOOK HER HEAD AND MUMBLED SOMETHING TO HERSELF BEFORE LETTING OUT A SLIGHT CHUCKLE. AS I LEFT MY POST, I WORRIED ABOUT MY DEAR FRIEND. SHE WAS CLEARLY JUST AS TROUBLED ABOUT THIS CASE AS I WAS CONFUSED ABOUT ANY INCLINATION OF WHO WAS RESPONSIBLE FOR MISS GARNER'S DISAPPEARANCE.

Chapter Three
"A Tale Told"

I FELT SICK IN MY STOMACH. SERGEANT COLLINS WAS RIGHT – TIME *WAS* RUNNING OUT AND WE HAD NO GUARANTEE OF MISS GARNER'S SAFETY OR WHEREABOUTS. IN FACT, WE HAD NOTHING. EVEN IF MISS GARNER WAS ALIVE NOW, WOULD SHE BE ALIVE WHEN WE FOUND HER, *IF* WE FOUND HER? I COULDN'T HELP BUT WONDER THAT, IF THIS WERE THE CASE, WOULD OUR POSTPONING THE SEARCH FOR THE NIGHT BE THE DIFFERENCE BETWEEN FINDING HER DEAD OR ALIVE? I DIDN'T SLEEP VERY WELL THAT NIGHT, DESPITE ALL OF MY TOSSING AND TURNING.

BY MORNING, I WAS STILL VERY WEARY AND HAD BEGUN TO DOUBT PENNY'S JUDGMENT ON THIS CASE. I COULDN'T RESIST THE NAGGING THOUGHT THAT THE REASON WHY PENNY DIDN'T WANT TO TALK ABOUT THE CASE WAS NOT BECAUSE SHE DIDN'T WANT TO GIVE ANYTHING AWAY, BUT BECAUSE SHE DIDN'T *HAVE* ANYTHING TO GIVE AWAY. I FELT FOR MY FRIEND, IT WAS, INDEED, A VERY DIFFICULT MYSTERY – ONE THAT SHE MIGHT NOT SOLVE. SHE WOULD NOT TAKE THAT WELL.

AFTER GETTING CHANGED AND FRESHENING UP, I WENT BACK TO THE RESTAURANT WE WERE IN THE PREVIOUS NIGHT THAT WAS NOW SET UP WITH A BUFFET BREAKFAST AND HOUSED THE STRONG SMELL OF FRESH HOT COFFEE THROUGHOUT THE ROOM. PENNY WAS ALREADY SITTING AT THE VERY SAME TABLE THAT WE WERE SEATED AT FOR DINNER, STROKING HER FINGER ALONG THE PAINTED PATTERN ON HER TEACUP. IT APPEARED THAT I HAD ALSO BEATEN THE MEN TO THE RESTAURANT. I GATHERED SOME FOOD AND A CUP OF TEA AND PLANTED MYSELF NEXT TO MY FRIEND.

"I TRUST THAT YOU SLEPT WELL?" I ASKED HER.

"OH, YES," SHE SMILED. "THAT BED WAS DIVINELY COMFORTABLE AND BREAKFAST WAS JUST THE CHERRY ON TOP OF THE CAKE. I SHALL HAVE TO STAY HERE AGAIN."

A FEW MOMENTS MORE OF PENNY RAVING ON ABOUT THE NICETIES OF THIS HOTEL PASSED AND WE WERE JOINED BY DETECTIVE WORTHINGTON AND SERGEANT COLLINS WHO APOLOGIZED FOR HIS OUTBURST THE NIGHT BEFORE. PENNY NODDED AND OFFERED HER FORGIVENESS.

"WAS THE STAY WORTHWHILE?" DETECTIVE WORTHINGTON DIRECTED HIS QUESTION TO PENNY.

"ABSOLUTELY," SHE SAID, NODDING HER HEAD. "I FEEL THAT I AM DEFINITELY MORE REFRESHED AND HAVE BEEN ABLE TO THOROUGHLY WEIGH UP EACH OF THE POSSIBILITIES FOR MISS GARNER'S KIDNAPPING."

"AND WHAT IS YOUR CONCLUSION?" HE SAID.

"I SAID THAT THEY HAVE BEEN WEIGHED," PENNY'S LIPS PURSED INTO A SMIRK. "I NEVER SAID THAT I HAD COME TO A CONCLUSION."

I CAST MY GAZE OVER TO SERGEANT COLLINS. AS I HAD SUSPECTED, PENNY'S STATEMENT SEEMED TO INFURIATE HIM – HIS EYE TWITCHED, HIS LIP QUIVERED SLIGHTLY AND HIS FISTS WERE CLENCHED. DESPITE HIS ANGER, HE DIDN'T SAY A WORD. PERHAPS DETECTIVE WORTHINGTON HAD UTILIZED THEIR TIME ALONE LAST NIGHT TO WARN HIM OF HIS ACTIONS. IT SEEMED THAT PENNY HAD THE SAME IDEA AS ME SINCE SHE APPEARED TO HAVE ALSO NOTICED SERGEANT COLLINS' DISCOMFORT.

"HOWEVER," SHE CONTINUED. "I DO KNOW WHERE WE WILL BE GOING NEXT."

"AND WHERE MIGHT THAT BE?" DETECTIVE WORTHINGTON SAID.

"BACK TO LONDON, OF COURSE," PENNY SAID MATTER-OF-FACTLY.

PENNY'S ANNOUNCEMENT SEEMED TO BE A BIT TOO MUCH FOR SERGEANT COLLINS TO HANDLE AND

HE LET HIS TEMPER GET THE BETTER OF HIM.

"BUT WHAT ABOUT LUTON?" HE SAID, HIS FISTS CLENCHED SO TIGHT THAT HIS KNUCKLES WERE WHITE.

"WHAT ABOUT IT?" PENNY SHRUGGED.

"DOESN'T IT SERVE ANY PURPOSE IN OUR INVESTIGATION?" HIS VOICE STARTED TO SHAKE AND HIS LIPS PRESSED INTO A SNARL. "OR WAS THE SOLE PURPOSE OF DRAGGING US ALL HERE FOR THE FOOD AND COMFORT?"

"ADMITTEDLY, THE FOOD AND COMFORT DID MAKE THIS TRIP DELIGHTFUL," SHE SAID. "BUT LUTON HAS NO PURPOSE FOR US NOW – MISS GARNER IS NOT HERE."

"HOW DO YOU KNOW?" SERGEANT COLLINS SAID, HIS FACE BEGINNING TO SOFTEN. "WHERE IS SHE?"

"JUST BECAUSE I SAY THAT SHE'S NOT HERE DOESN'T MEAN THAT I KNOW EXACTLY WHERE SHE IS," SHE RESPONDED, SQUINTING HER EYES AT SERGEANT COLLINS. "IT SIMPLY MEANS THAT SHE IS NOT HERE."

ONCE AGAIN, THE YOUNG SERGEANT'S FACE HARDENED AND HE THREW HIS ARMS IN THE AIR.

"DO YOU THINK THIS IS ALL A GAME?" HE YELLED. SERGEANT COLLINS STOOD UP FROM HIS CHAIR AND LEANED ACROSS THE TABLE SO THAT HIS FACE WAS MERE INCHES FROM PENNY'S, DETECTIVE WORTHINGTON GRASPING ONTO HIS ARM AS A PREVENTATIVE.

"MISS GARNER'S LIFE COULD BE IN DANGER AND YOU TREAT IT AS THOUGH IT'S A GAME," HE CONTINUED, HIS VOICE NOW ONLY LOUD ENOUGH FOR THE THREE OF US TO HEAR IT. "*MISS FINKLE*, I HAVE HAD IT WITH YOUR GAMES. I WAS RIGHT WHEN I SAID THAT WE SHOULD NOT CONSULT YOU, BUT DETECTIVE WORTHINGTON ASSURED ME THAT YOU WERE THE BEST PERSON FOR THIS JOB. WELL, HE WAS WRONG! AND NOW, WE ARE EXACTLY WHERE WE STARTED

EXCEPT WITH A TWO-HOUR TRIP AHEAD OF US. WE HAVE *NOTHING* – AND YOU KNOW IT!"

"SERGEANT COLLINS," DETECTIVE WORTHINGTON WARNED.

HE LOOKED AT THE DETECTIVE AND AROUND THE ROOM WHERE EVERYONE SEEMED TO HAVE STOPPED WHAT THEY WERE DOING TO WATCH THE SCENE THAT WAS UNFOLDING IN FRONT OF THEM. UNBEKNOWN TO HIM, HIS VOICE HAD GROWN LOUDER THROUGHOUT HIS BLUSTER. HE STRAIGHTENED HIS SHIRT AND SEATED HIMSELF BACK DOWN, HIS ATTENTION DRAWN BACK TO PENNY AT THE SOUND OF HER VOICE.

"MR COLLINS," SHE SAID, HER EYEBROW RAISED. "IF I AM JUDGING CORRECTLY, IT WOULD SEEM THAT YOU CARE DEEPLY FOR MISS GARNER. AM I CORRECT?"

SERGEANT COLLINS LOOKED AGHAST AT THE SUGGESTION, HIS LIPS PRESSED TIGHTLY TOGETHER. THOUGH HE DIDN'T DENY IT – IN FACT, HE DIDN'T SAY ANYTHING AT ALL. HE JUST SAT VERY STILL, ONE HAND HOLDING TIGHTLY TO THE GLASS OF WATER IN FRONT OF HIM AND THE OTHER HAND TRACING THE EDGE OF THE PLATE. I SAW HIS LIP QUIVER EVER SO SLIGHTLY AND HIS EYES GREW GLASSY. HIS JAW WAS CLENCHED AND HE SWALLOWED NERVOUSLY.

"JUST AS I THOUGHT," PENNY SIGHED. "DID YOU KNOW ABOUT THIS?" SHE ASKED THE DETECTIVE.

DETECTIVE WORTHINGTON SHOOK HIS HEAD – HE LOOKED ALMOST AS SHOCKED AND SPEECHLESS AS HIS ACQUAINTANCE. ALTHOUGH WE HAD ALL REMAINED OBLIVIOUS TO THIS FACT, PENNY HAD MANAGED TO PICK UP ON WHAT WE COULD NOT SEE. ONCE AGAIN, MY FAITH WAS RESTORED IN MY FRIEND'S ABILITY – IF ANYONE COULD SOLVE THIS MYSTERY, IT WOULD BE HER.

"DO YOU CARE TO EXPLAIN, OR SHALL I?" SHE SAID, DIRECTING HER QUESTION TO SERGEANT COLLINS.

"WAIT A MOMENT," DETECTIVE WORTHINGTON INTERJECTED, SHAKING HIS HEAD. "YOU DON'T THINK

THAT SERGEANT COLLINS HAS ANYTHING TO DO WITH MISS GARNER BEING MISSING, DO YOU?"

"OF COURSE NOT," PENNY GASPED, SHOCKED OF SUCH AN ACCUSATION. "BUT HE DID KEEP THIS IMPORTANT PIECE OF INFORMATION FROM YOU."

WE SAT IN SILENCE FOR A MOMENT OR TWO, WAITING FOR THE NEXT PERSON TO MAKE THEIR MOVE. FINALLY, DETECTIVE WORTHINGTON BROKE THE SILENCE, ASKING HIS ACQUAINTANCE WHY HE DIDN'T TELL HIM THAT HE CARED FOR HER.

"I THOUGHT THAT YOU WOULDN'T KEEP ME ON THE CASE IF YOU KNEW THAT I CARED FOR HER," SERGEANT COLLINS EXPLAINED QUIETLY.

"WELL, YOU THOUGHT CORRECTLY," DETECTIVE WORTHINGTON SAID. "WHEN WE GET BACK TO LONDON, YOU'RE OFF THE CASE. I'LL GET SOMEONE ELSE ON, INSTEAD."

"SIR, PLEASE," HE SAID, HIS EYES PLEADING. "I COULDN'T TRUST ANYONE ELSE TO FIND HER."

"HE'S RIGHT," PENNY SAID. "EVEN THOUGH HE LET HIS FEELINGS GET IN THE WAY OF THE INVESTIGATION, NOW THAT WE KNOW ABOUT IT, IT COULD COME IN USEFUL."

"VERY WELL," DETECTIVE WORTHINGTON SAID. "IT'S AGAINST PROTOCOL, BUT I'LL MAKE AN EXCEPTION."

"NOW," PENNY CONTINUED. "HOW DID YOU COME TO CARE FOR MISS GARNER?"

"I DON'T SEE HOW HEARING ABOUT HIS INTEREST IN MISS GARNER IS GOING TO HELP THE INVESTIGATION," THE DETECTIVE SAID, PENNY SHUSHING HIM BEFORE HE COULD CONTINUE.

"WELL," SERGEANT COLLINS BEGAN. "WE GREW UP TOGETHER. I WAS GOOD FRIENDS WITH HER BROTHER FOR MANY YEARS – WE ALWAYS PLAYED TOGETHER WHEN WE HAD A CHANCE AND EILEEN OFTEN JOINED IN. HER BROTHER DIED FROM INFLUENZA WHEN HE WAS SIXTEEN, BUT EILEEN AND I STILL REMAINED

CLOSE. FOUR YEARS AFTER HER BROTHER DIED, I TOLD HER THAT I LOVED HER AND WISHED TO COURT HER – AND WE DID, FOR A YEAR OR SO. THEN SHE BROKE IT OFF BECAUSE SHE WANTED TO CHASE DOWN HER DREAM OF BECOMING AN ACTRESS. IT BROKE

MY HEART," HIS GLASSY EYES SHONE AS HE CONTINUED TO STARE AT THE WATER. "I SHOULD NEVER HAVE LET HER GO, BUT I DID. I'VE NEVER STOPPED REGRETTING IT. WHEN I HEARD THAT SHE WAS GOING TO BE STARRING IN A FILM IN LONDON, I COULDN'T WAIT TO SEE HER AGAIN AND TELL HER."
"THAT YOU WANT TO BE TOGETHER AGAIN," I SAID, DABBING MY WEEPING EYES WITH A HANDKERCHIEF.

SERGEANT COLLINS NODDED. WE SAT IN SILENCE FOR A MOMENT LONGER BEFORE GATHERING OUR THINGS AND HEADING OUT TO THE CAR. I FELT FOR SERGEANT COLLINS AND UNDERSTOOD COMPLETELY WHY HE KEPT HIS FEELINGS HIDDEN FROM US. PERHAPS IT WAS A WAY THAT HE THOUGHT HE COULD MAKE UP WITH HER, BY BEING A PART OF THE INVESTIGATION IN FINDING HER. AT LEAST ONE THING WAS FOR CERTAIN – HE WOULDN'T BE GIVING UP ON IT. AS WE CLIMBED INTO THE CAR, SERGEANT COLLINS SEEMED TO BE IN A BETTER MOOD – THAT WAS, UNTIL HE ASKED PENNY THE ONE THING THAT WAS ON HIS MIND.

"SO," HE SAID. "WHO ARE WE GOING TO FIND IN LONDON?"

"WE'RE GOING TO SEE HER SISTER," PENNY SAID RELUCTANTLY.

"MISS GARNER DOESN'T HAVE A SISTER," HE INTERJECTED, HIS TONE ONCE MORE CONFUSED.

"OH YES, SHE DOES," PENNY SAID.

Chapter Four
"The Photograph"

OUR TWO-HOUR TRIP BACK TO LONDON WAS, ONCE AGAIN, FILLED WITH SILENCE, BUT THAT DIDN'T BOTHER ME – NOR DID IT SEEM TO BOTHER PENNY WHO WAS SITTING BESIDE ME WITH HER EYES CLOSED. I TOOK IN ALL THE DETAILS OF THE MORNING SO FAR. EVEN THOUGH I DIDN'T KNOW WHERE MISS GARNER WAS OR WHO WAS RESPONSIBLE, I COULD SEE HOW VISITING HER SISTER MIGHT HELP WITH DEVELOPING AN IDEA OF WHO SHE MIGHT BE WITH – A SISTER THAT SERGEANT COLLINS SEEMED TO KNOW NOTHING ABOUT. IT MADE ME WONDER, THOUGH, THAT IF SERGEANT COLLINS HAD BEEN SO CLOSE TO MISS GARNER, HOW HAD HE NOT KNOWN ABOUT HER SISTER?

MY THOUGHTS THEN DELVED INTO OUR LIST OF SUSPECTS THAT STILL, AS FAR AS I KNEW, CONSISTED OF ONLY ONE PERSON – MR ERNEST SNIEDER. I WONDERED HOW WE WOULD FIND HIM. ALL THAT WE KNEW ABOUT HIM WAS THAT HE WAS JUST A SNEAKY CAMERAMAN WITH A GRUDGE WHO NO ONE ON THE SET SEEMED TO HAVE A DEEP FRIENDSHIP WITH OR KNEW MUCH ABOUT AT ALL. IT WAS AS THOUGH NO ONE EVEN CARED A THOUGHT FOR HIM – HE HAD NOTHING TO LOSE. HOPEFULLY, MISS GARNER'S SISTER WILL GIVE US ALL THE INFORMATION THAT WE NEED.

I DIDN'T PAY MUCH ATTENTION AS TO WHERE IN LONDON WE WERE ACTUALLY GOING, I JUST HOPED THAT WE WERE COMING UP TO THE FINAL RUN SINCE THE REST OF THE INVESTIGATION FELT LIKE WE WERE GOING AROUND IN CIRCLES. EVENTUALLY, WE CAME TO OUR DESTINATION. AS PENNY AND MYSELF CLIMBED OUT OF THE CAR, I OVERHEARD PENNY INSTRUCT DETECTIVE WORTHINGTON TO CALL THE STATION AND SEE IF HE COULD GET ANOTHER CAR TO

JOIN US. THEN, PENNY AND I MARCHED OUR WAY UP TO THE BIG TIMBER DOOR, KNOCKED AND WAITED. AFTER A MOMENT, WE HEARD FOOTSTEPS CREAKING CLOSER TO THE DOOR BEFORE A WOMAN APPEARED WHO LOOKED JUST LIKE THE PICTURES I HAD SEEN OF MISS GARNER. I WAS SHOCKED AT FIRST – HAD WE JUST FOUND MISS GARNER? SEEMINGLY, PENNY THOUGHT OTHERWISE.

"MRS BETTY HUNT?" PENNY SAID TO THE WOMAN.
"YES," THE WOMAN REPLIED. "AND WHO ARE YOU?"
"I'M PENELOPE FINKLE AND THIS IS MY DEAR FRIEND, MISS ANDREA WRIGHT," SHE SAID, HER EYES GLEAMING. "WE'RE LOOKING FOR YOUR SISTER – MISS GARNER."
"WELL, YOU WOULD PROBABLY FIND HER ON SET," MRS HUNT SAID. "SHE'S NOT HERE."

PENNY AND I SHARED A KNOWING LOOK BEFORE PENNY CAST A CONCERNED EYE ON THE WOMAN IN FRONT OF US.

"SHE DOESN'T KNOW," I WHISPERED, REALIZATION HITTING ME.

SHE IS MISS GARNER'S SISTER AND NO ONE CARED TO TELL HER THAT SHE WAS MISSING. THOUGH, SHE IS A SISTER THAT PERHAPS NO ONE KNEW ABOUT.

"KNOW WHAT?" MRS HUNT SAID, HER FACE FROZEN WITH TERROR. "WHY ARE YOU LOOKING FOR EILEEN?"
"MRS HUNT," PENNY BEGAN. "PERHAPS WE HAD BETTER COME IN."

MRS HUNT STOOD ASIDE TO LET US THROUGH THE DOOR. THE HALLWAY WAS LONG AND DIMLY LIT, FEATURING A TALL COAT STAND AND A LONG TAPESTRY RUG. SHE LED US TO THE END OF THE HALLWAY WHERE THE KITCHEN AND DINING TABLE WERE SITUATED AND OFFERED US TEA. WE ACCEPTED THE TEA AND SEATED OURSELVES AT THE DINING TABLE. A TALL THIN VASE WITH THREE FRESH ROSES – TWO RED ROSES AND ONE PINK ROSE – SAT ON A DELICATE DOILY IN THE MIDDLE OF THE SMALL TABLE.

When Mrs Hunt joined us at the table, Penny began to explain the situation to her.

"We suspect that Miss Garner has been kidnapped," she said, slightly hesitant.

"Who do you think is responsible?" Mrs Hunt said, her face pale as snow.

"We don't know," Penny sighed. "We were hoping that you might know if there was someone who may have a grudge against her."

Mrs Hunt shook her head.

"What makes you think that I would know anything?" she said.

"Well, you are her sister," I said.

"Not many people know that fact," her face grew even paler and her lips tightened. "How did you come across this information?"

"What else would people think you are to her?" I said. "The resemblance is uncanny – are you twins?"

"How we found out that you are both so closely related is irrelevant," Penny said. "What truly matters is that Miss Garner is missing and we're trying to put the pieces of the puzzle together."

Mrs Hunt traced her finger along the pattern of the delicate doily, eying it studiously. Finally, she took a sip of her tea and sighed.

"How can I be of help?" she said.

Penny clasped her hands together and smiled. "Are you close to Miss Garner?" she began.

"Oh, yes," Mrs Hunt said. "We try to see each other as often as possible."

"So, you would share a lot of things with each other?" Penny said.

"Everything," she replied.

"Do you know if Miss Garner ever had a

RELATIONSHIP WITH MR ROBERT COLLINS?" PENNY ASKED.

I LOOKED AT PENNY, SURPRISED THAT SHE ASKED THIS QUESTION. DID SHE, TOO, SUSPECT THAT SERGEANT COLLINS MIGHT HAVE SOMETHING TO DO WITH MISS GARNER'S DISAPPEARANCE? I WONDERED IF THAT WAS WHY SHE WANTED TO SEE MRS HUNT – TO SEE IF SERGEANT COLLINS' STORY WAS TRUE. MRS HUNT'S BROW WAS FURROWED AND HER EYES NARROWED. AFTER A MOMENT, SHE LEANED BACK IN HER CHAIR AND RUBBED THE BACK OF HER NECK WITH ONE HAND.

"I DON'T RECOLLECT ANY MENTION OF THAT NAME," SHE FINALLY SAID, FIXING HER GAZE, ONCE AGAIN, ON THE DOILY.

"MRS HUNT," PENNY SAID, LEANING FORWARD. "THIS WOULD NOT HAVE BEEN A RECENT RELATIONSHIP. SHE WOULD HAVE BEEN EIGHTEEN WHEN IT HAPPENED."

"SHE DID TELL ME – ONCE – ABOUT A MAN SHE LEFT BEHIND WHEN SHE STARTING CHASING HER ACTING CAREER," SHE SAID HESITANTLY.

"OH?" PENNY RAISED HER EYEBROW. "WHAT DID SHE SAY?"

"WELL," MRS HUNT CONTINUED. "SHE SAID THAT SHE HAD SEEN HIM AROUND AND SHE HOPED THAT THEY WOULD RECONNECT. THEN, NOT LONG AFTER, SHE BROUGHT A MAN OVER TO INTRODUCE TO MY HUSBAND AND I. WE ASSUMED THAT HE WAS THE MAN SHE LEFT BEHIND. HIS NAME ISN'T ROBERT COLLINS, THOUGH."

"WHAT IS HIS NAME?" PENNY ASKED, RUBBING HER HANDS TOGETHER.

"PETER BOURKE," SHE SAID, SQUINTING AT PENNY.

"ARE THEY STILL TOGETHER?" PENNY QUESTIONED.

"NO," MRS HUNT SAID, DROPPING HER HANDS INTO HER LAP. "THEY ENDED IT MONTHS AGO. THEY WERE TOGETHER FOR A WHILE, THOUGH – ALMOST A YEAR.

He used to come and visit us, you know, before she ended it with him. We haven't seen him since. It's a shame really. We all liked him; he was a true gentleman." Mrs Hunt crossed her arms and closed her eyes for a moment. "She never should have left him, as far as I am concerned."

"Why did she end it with him, Mrs Hunt?" Penny said, leaning back into her chair.

"He proposed to her," Mrs Hunt said.

"And she said no," I finished, receiving a nod from Mrs Hunt. "Why?"

"She has commitment issues, I suppose," Mrs Hunt shrugged. "She doesn't want to give up her acting career."

"I don't suppose you could describe what he looks like?" Penny asked, tilting her head to one side.

"I can do one better," Mrs Hunt said, her finger raised in front of us as she left her chair and went to the kitchen cupboard. "Eileen made us give her every photograph that we had of him so that she could destroy them," she shuffled all the cups in the highest shelf before coming across an envelope that had a clear purpose of hiding something. "I kept my favorite, though. She wouldn't be very happy if she knew I kept it."

I saw an awry grin appear across Mrs Hunt's face as she handed the photograph to Penny. I leaned over to see the picture. A woman, who must have been Miss Garner, was standing next to a tall, dark-haired man who I assumed was Mr Bourke. He had his arm around her and she was leaning close to him, looking up at his face with a big smile across her own. It was unmistakeable that they were happy. I smiled at the photograph; I could see why Mrs Hunt liked him – they seemed to be a perfect fit. My

GAZE DRIFTED TO THE BACKGROUND OF THE PHOTO. THEY WERE STANDING ON THE PORCH OF WHAT APPEARED TO BE A LOG CABIN. TO THE RIGHT OF THE PHOTOGRAPH WERE DENSE TREES AND BUSH. IT SEEMED THAT PENNY HAD THE SAME QUESTION AS ME.
"WHERE WAS THIS PHOTOGRAPH TAKEN?" SHE ASKED.
"I'LL NEVER FORGET THAT PLACE," MRS HUNT SAID, HER MIND WANDERING INTO A MEMORY. "HE INVITED US ALL TO A PLACE JUST OUTSIDE OF HORSHAM FOR THE WEEKEND – ABOUT TWO HOURS SOUTH OF HERE. THAT'S WHERE HE ASKED MY HUSBAND AND I FOR PERMISSION TO PROPOSE TO EILEEN. WE GAVE IT TO HIM, OF COURSE, AND HE PROPOSED TO HER THE NEXT DAY."
I SAW A TEAR WELL UP IN MRS HUNT'S LEFT EYE AS SHE REACHED INTO HER APRON POCKET TO FIND A HANDKERCHIEF.
"HE WANTED TO DO IT THERE," SHE CONTINUED ONCE SHE HAD COMPOSED HERSELF. "IT WAS A CABIN THAT HE WAS PLANNING ON BUYING FROM A FRIEND OF HIS. IT WAS GOING TO BE THEIR HOME. I DON'T BELIEVE HE EVER GOT IT AFTER THAT."
"DO YOU REMEMBER HOW TO GET THERE?" PENNY SAID, POINTING TO THE PHOTOGRAPH.
"I COULDN'T DESCRIBE IT," SHE SAID. "BUT I WOULD REMEMBER MY WAY IF I WAS THERE AGAIN."
PENNY HANDED THE PHOTOGRAPH BACK TO MRS HUNT AND STOOD FROM HER CHAIR. TO MY SURPRISE, SHE ASKED MRS HUNT IF SHE WOULD BE ABLE TO COME WITH US FOR THE REMAINDER OF THE INVESTIGATION AND MRS HUNT AGREED.
"ANYTHING WOULD BE BETTER THAN SITTING IDLY BY WITHOUT KNOWING WHERE SHE IS," MRS HUNT SAID.
THE THREE OF US GATHERED OUR PURSES AND COATS AND MADE OUR WAY OUTSIDE. I DIDN'T KNOW HOW LONG WE HAD BEEN INSIDE TALKING TO MRS

HUNT, BUT BY THE TIME WE WERE OUTSIDE, THERE WAS A POLICE CAR SITUATED BEHIND THE DETECTIVE'S ASTON MARTIN AND ANOTHER POLICEMAN TALKING TO DETECTIVE WORTHINGTON AND SERGEANT COLLINS. THIS MAN, WHOM DETECTIVE WORTHINGTON INTRODUCED AS CONSTABLE BENNETT, LOOKED TO BE IN HIS FORTIES WITH A TALL STRONG BUILD AND GRAYING HAIR. IN JUST A FEW MOMENTS, THE SEATING ARRANGEMENTS WERE PLANNED. DETECTIVE WORTHINGTON, PENNY AND MRS HUNT WERE TO GO IN FRONT OF THE POLICE CAR IN THE ASTON MARTIN, WHILE I WAS TO GO IN THE POLICE CAR WITH SERGEANT COLLINS AND CONSTABLE BENNETT. I ASSUMED THAT THIS ARRANGEMENT WAS PARTLY BECAUSE OF MRS HUNT BEING QUESTIONED ABOUT SERGEANT COLLINS.

I STILL DIDN'T FULLY UNDERSTAND WHY PENNY INSISTED THAT MRS HUNT CAME ON THE INVESTIGATION – NOR DID I KNOW IF PENNY INTENDED ON ASKING HER MORE QUESTIONS IN THE CAR. ONE THING WAS FOR SURE, THOUGH – PENNY WOULD NOT HAVE ASKED DETECTIVE WORTHINGTON TO SOURCE A SECOND CAR IF SHE DIDN'T KNOW THAT WE WERE CLOSE TO FINDING MISS GARNER.

Chapter Five
"An Untraveled Road"

THE ROAD WE TOOK WAS FAMILIAR TO ME AS IT SEEMED TO BE THE SAME ROAD THAT WE TOOK TO GO TO THE SET THE PREVIOUS DAY. I WONDERED IF PENNY NEEDED TO ASK MORE QUESTIONS TO SOMEONE THERE OR WHETHER SHE THOUGHT MISS GARNER WAS ACTUALLY STILL ON SET. AS I CONSCIOUSLY PREPARED FOR THE CARS TO TURN INTO THE SET, I WAS SURPRISED THAT THEY DIDN'T. THE ASTON MARTIN WENT STRAIGHT PAST THE FRONT GATE AND CONTINUED DOWN THE ROAD.

A NUMBER OF TURNS LED THROUGH A PART OF LONDON THAT I HAD NOT BEEN THROUGH BEFORE WHICH DELVED MY MIND INTO A STATE OF CONFUSION AS TO WHICH DIRECTION WE WERE HEADED. SOON ENOUGH, WE HAD LEFT LONDON AND WERE HEADED DOWN AN OLD ROAD THAT WAS NEW TO ME. I WONDERED HOW PENNY HAD KNOWN THAT MISS GARNER HAD A SISTER. COULD IT HAVE BEEN FROM THE MAN THAT I SAW HER TALKING TO OUTSIDE THE TRAILERS? OR, PERHAPS, SHE GOT THE INFORMATION

FROM OUR TRIP TO LUTON. I STILL DIDN'T UNDERSTAND OUR TRIP TO LUTON, THOUGH. IT SEEMED TO BE A WASTE OF TIME. I NEVER SAW HER TALK TO ANYONE OR LOOK FOR ANYTHING AND I WAS ALWAYS WITH HER. EXCEPT, OF COURSE, WHEN WE WERE IN OUR SEPARATE ROOMS AND WHEN I BID HER GOODNIGHT, LEAVING HER TO ONE MORE POT OF TEA, BUT NO ONE ELSE WAS IN THE RESTAURANT OTHER

THAN THE STAFF.

NUMEROUS THOUGHTS SPUN IN MY MIND, CONFUSING ME MORE THAN I ALREADY WAS. I WONDERED ABOUT WHO PENNY THOUGHT WAS RESPONSIBLE FOR MISS GARNER'S DISAPPEARANCE – WAS IT TRULY MR SNIEDER? IF SO, HOW DID SHE COME TO THE CONCLUSION AS TO WHERE HE WOULD BE? WAS IT, PERHAPS, SOMEONE THAT I HAD NOT YET CONSIDERED? WE TRAVELED FOR ABOUT TWO HOURS BEFORE DRIVING THROUGH A SMALL MARKET TOWN AND PULLING OVER IN FRONT OF A CABIN THAT I EXPECTED WAS THE SAME CABIN IN THE PHOTOGRAPH THAT MRS HUNT SHOWED US EARLIER. MAYBE PENNY THOUGHT THERE MIGHT BE A LINK BETWEEN MR SNIEDER AND THIS CABIN.

BEFORE I WAS ABLE TO GET OUT OF THE CAR, I NOTICED THAT DETECTIVE WORTHINGTON WAS THE ONLY ONE TO LEAVE THE ASTON MARTIN. HE CAME OVER TO THE POLICE CAR AND ASKED SERGEANT COLLINS AND CONSTABLE BENNETT TO JOIN HIM BUT, AS INSTRUCTED, I STAYED IN THE CAR. I COULDN'T SEE WHAT WAS HAPPENING VERY WELL AS THE PATH FROM THE CAR TO THE CABIN WAS HIDDEN BETWEEN TREES. AFTER A FEW MINUTES, SERGEANT COLLINS BROUGHT A DISILLUSIONED MAN BACK TO OUR CAR WHO HE INTRODUCED AS MR ERNEST SNIEDER. I WAS SO CONCENTRATED ON MR SNIEDER BEING IN THE CAR THAT I ONLY CAUGHT A SHORT GLIMPSE OF TWO OTHER PEOPLE ENTERING THE ASTON MARTIN IN FRONT OF US – A MAN AND A WOMAN. I ASSUMED THAT THE WOMAN WAS MISS GARNER, THOUGH I DID NOT KNOW WHO THE MAN WAS. IT SEEMED THAT MR SNIEDER WAS WHO PENNY THOUGHT WAS RESPONSIBLE FOR THE KIDNAPPING – AN OBVIOUS

SUSPECT, CONSIDERING HIS HISTORY.

WE WERE, ONCE MORE, ON THE ROAD AGAIN. THIS TIME, BACK TO LONDON. FOR THE TWO-HOUR TRIP BACK, I COULDN'T HELP BUT NOTICE THAT MR SNIEDER SMELT OF ANXIOUS SWEAT AND HIS CLOTHES WERE TATTERED AND DIRTY. HE KEPT HIS GAZE FIXED ON THE SEAT IN FRONT OF HIM. I COULDN'T EVEN IMAGINE WHAT THOUGHTS MAY HAVE BEEN GOING THROUGH HIS HEAD AND I WONDERED WHAT INTENTIONS HE HAD FOR KIDNAPPING MISS GARNER. AFTER WHAT SEEMED LIKE A VERY LONG DRIVE, WE FINALLY TURNED INTO THE SET OF *PASSION IN LONDON*. IT APPEARED AS THOUGH THIS MYSTERY WAS FINALLY COMING TO A CLOSE.

ONCE THE CARS HAD STOPPED, EVERYONE EMPTIED OUT OF THEM EXCEPT FOR THE MAN IN THE ASTON MARTIN WHO, I NOTICED, WAS HANDCUFFED AND RECOGNIZED HIM AS THE MAN IN THE PHOTOGRAPH – MR PETER BOURKE. I DID NOTICE, HOWEVER, THAT MR SNIEDER WAS NOT HANDCUFFED AND WAS SIMPLY REQUESTED TO STAY AND PROVIDE A STATEMENT. MR SNIEDER APPEARED TO BE INNOCENT AFTER ALL. THE WOMAN WHO WAS IN THE CAR WAS, INDEED, MISS GARNER WHO WAS NOW BEING CONSOLED BY MRS HUNT AND SERGEANT COLLINS. I FOLLOWED PENNY AND DETECTIVE WORTHINGTON FURTHER INTO THE SET WHERE WE MANAGED TO FIND MISS GARNER'S UNDERSTUDY.

"MISS HENRIETTA BROWNLEY," DETECTIVE WORTHINGTON SAID. "YOU ARE UNDER ARREST FOR THE KIDNAPPING OF MISS EILEEN GARNER."

ALONG WITH MANY OTHERS ON THE SET, I WAS VERY SURPRISED AT THIS ARREST. ALTHOUGH I DID NOT SEE IT COMING, PENNY OBVIOUSLY FELT THAT MISS BROWNLEY PLAYED A SIGNIFICANT ROLE IN MISS GARNER'S KIDNAPPING. I COULDN'T WAIT TO ASK HER.

After the arrests had been made, statements were taken and Miss Garner had thanked us all profusely, Detective Worthington and Sergeant Collins drove us back to Penny's house. As we stood on her doorstep, Sergeant Collins asked Penny the one question that I was eager to ask.

"Miss Finkle, if I may," he said. "How did you know that it was Miss Brownley and Mr Bourke?"

Penny let a deep and sincere smile take over her face as she prepared herself to tell her story. She reached into her purse and pulled out the scrunched papers from Mrs Hodgkins and the paper that I recognized as the one that Miss Brownley had autographed.

"When someone is kidnapped," she began. "There is almost certainly more than one person involved. It didn't take me long to figure out that Miss Brownley was probably involved, but I had to find who else was involved in order to find Miss Garner. See, Miss Brownley seemed to care for Miss Garner much more than an understudy usually would."

"How did you figure that?" Sergeant Collins said.

"The man outside of the trailer?" I asked. Penny nodded at me, her eyes gleaming with the thrill of recounting the events.

"He was the understudy for the male leading role of the film," she continued. "Miss Brownley mentioned something that made me wonder about her sincerity. She said that understudies were the stars' biggest friends and support. Though, when I asked this man, he said that all understudies have a professional relationship with the leads, though, deep down, they always hope that the lead won't be

ABLE TO ACT WHEN FILMING STARTS. HE SAID, 'WE'RE ALL IN THIS FOR THE SAME THING – OUR LOVE OF ACTING. UNDERSTUDIES GET THEIR BIG BREAKS WHEN A LEAD IS NOT ABLE TO ACT.'"

"MISS BROWNLEY WANTED HER BIG BREAK," DETECTIVE WORTHINGTON SAID, SMILING AND SHAKING HIS HEAD.

PENNY'S EYES DANCED AND SHE CLASPED HER HANDS TOGETHER AS SHE CONTINUED.

"PRECISELY," SHE SAID. "AND, EVEN THOUGH HER TRAILER DIDN'T OFFER MUCH, I FOUND AN ADDRESS BOOK HIDDEN UNDERNEATH HER PILLOW WITH THE ADDRESS OF THE PLACE WE WENT TO IN LUTON LISTED UNDER 'A'. NOW, IT MADE SENSE THAT EMERGENCY CONTACTS ARE WRITTEN FIRST IN ADDRESS BOOKS, THOUGH I WASN'T YET INTENDING TO TRAVEL THERE. OUR NEXT STOP WAS, OF COURSE, TO SEE MRS

HODGKINS WHO HAD SOME VERY USEFUL INFORMATION FOR US – A LETTER AND THE ACCOMPANYING ENVELOPE. THE FIRST THING I NOTICED WAS THAT THE RETURN ADDRESS ON THE ENVELOPE WAS THE ADDRESS OF WHERE WE WERE YET TO STAY IN LUTON – THE VERY SAME ADDRESS THAT WAS WRITTEN FIRST IN THE ADDRESS BOOK. THE LETTER SAID THAT HER AUNTY HAD FALLEN TERRIBLY ILL AND SHE WAS NEEDED IN LUTON TO BE WITH HER. HOWEVER," SHE WAVED A FINGER IN FRONT OF HER FACE BEFORE POINTING TO THE INSIGNIA STAMPED ON THE FRONT OF THE ENVELOPE. "THIS LETTER WAS SENT FROM LONDON, NOT LUTON, AND THE HANDWRITING WAS INCREDIBLY SIMILAR TO MISS BROWNLEY'S HANDWRITING ON THE AUTOGRAPH THAT I MANAGED TO GET FROM HER."

PENNY UNFOLDED THE PAPER WITH THE AUTOGRAPH AND SHOWED US THE COMPARISON BETWEEN THE AUTOGRAPH AND THE LETTER.

"SEE," SHE THEN CONTINUED. "IF MISS

BROWNLEY'S DECEPTION HAD WORKED, THEN THE KIDNAPPING MAY NOT HAVE BEEN NECESSARY AS MISS GARNER WOULD HAVE BEEN IN LUTON WITH HER AUNTY. BUT IT SEEMED AS THOUGH MISS GARNER KNEW BETTER AND ASKED HER SISTER WHO DENIED SUCH AN ILLNESS, WHICH MRS HUNT CONFESSED ON OUR WAY TO HORSHAM. THEY ARE TWINS, YES, THOUGH THEIR MOTHER WAS ILL WHEN THEY WERE YOUNG, SO THEIR AUNTY TOOK PRIMARY CARE OF MRS HUNT TO HELP AS MUCH AS SHE COULD. THEY ONLY DISCOVERED THAT THEY WERE, INDEED, SISTERS AFTER MISS GARNER HAD STARTED ACTING – EXPLAINING THE REASON WHY YOU DID NOT KNOW THAT SHE HAD A SISTER."
SHE INDICATED SERGEANT COLLINS WHO NODDED HIS HEAD DEEPLY IN REALIZATION.
"BUT WE DIDN'T KNOW THAT SHE HAD A SISTER, EITHER, UNTIL OUR TRIP TO LUTON WHERE I WAS ABLE TO TALK TO MISS GARNER'S AUNTY – WHO MANAGED THE HOTEL – AND CONFIRMING THAT SHE WAS NOT ILL. SHE LET ME KNOW ABOUT MRS HUNT."
"HOW DID YOU KNOW THAT PETER BOURKE WAS INVOLVED?" I ASKED MY DEAR FRIEND.
"THAT WAS EASY," SHE SMILED FROM EAR TO EAR. "WHEN I TALKED TO THE MAN OUTSIDE OF THE TRAILER, HE SAID THAT HE HAD SEEN MISS BROWNLEY WITH A MAN NAMED PETER. HE SAID IT WAS ALL VERY SECRETIVE, BUT HE HEARD A RUMOR THAT THEY WERE TOGETHER. HE DESCRIBED THE MAN TO ME WHICH MATCHED THE APPEARANCE OF PETER BOURKE IN THE PHOTOGRAPH. HE OBVIOUSLY HAD HURT FEELINGS TOWARDS MISS GARNER SINCE SHE TURNED DOWN HIS PROPOSAL AND A MAN OF HIS DESCRIPTION HAD BEEN SECRETLY SEEING MISS BROWNLEY. IT MADE SENSE THAT HE COULD BE INVOLVED AND WOULD BE DIFFICULT TO LINK WITH THE KIDNAPPING – THOUGH, NOT FOR ME, OF COURSE. I FIGURED THAT HE WOULD

TAKE HER TO THE CABIN WHERE IT WOULD REMIND HER OF HOW SHE BROKE HIS HEART."

"BUT WHAT ABOUT MR SNIEDER?" DETECTIVE WORTHINGTON ASKED. "HOW DID YOU KNOW THAT HE DIDN'T DO IT?"

"MR SNIEDER MAY HAVE BEEN SNEAKY AND HAD A BAD REPUTATION," SHE SHRUGGED. "BUT HE WAS NOT INVOLVED. HE WAS SIMPLY THE IDEAL PERSON TO FRAME THE KIDNAPPING ON. WHEN YOU SAID THAT HE, TOO, WAS MISSING, I FIGURED THAT MR SNIEDER HAD ALSO BEEN KIDNAPPED AND, THEREFORE, ALSO NEEDED TO BE FOUND. THE BEST WAY OF FINDING MR SNIEDER WAS TO FIND MISS GARNER."

"MISS FINKLE," SERGEANT COLLINS SAID. "HOW DID YOU KNOW THAT MISS GARNER'S LIFE WASN'T IN DANGER?"

"*SERGEANT* COLLINS," SHE SAID, SMILING AT THE YOUNG MAN. "MISS BROWNLEY WANTED HER BIG BREAK – NOT TO CAUSE HARM TO MISS GARNER. AS THE DIRECTOR, MR POSTLETHWAITE, SAID, THEY WERE ON A VERY TIGHT SCHEDULE. ALL THAT MISS BROWNLEY HAD TO DO WAS KEEP MISS GARNER AWAY FROM THE SET FOR LONG ENOUGH FOR THEM TO START FILMING WITH MISS BROWNLEY AS THE FEMALE LEAD. ONCE FILMING HAD STARTED, THERE WOULD BE NO TIME TO RESTART FILMING. THE BIGGEST DANGER THAT MISS GARNER WAS IN WAS THE FACT THAT SHE WAS DRUGGED TO GET HER THERE."

"THE GLASS ON THE SINK," I SAID.

PENNY NODDED, HOLDING HER HEAD HIGH AND SMILING AT THE THREE OF US. I KNEW THAT I SHOULD NEVER HAVE DOUBTED PENNY'S ABILITY AND I, TOO, WAS PROUD OF HER FOR SOLVING THIS MYSTERY.

"WELL," DETECTIVE WORTHINGTON SAID. "ANOTHER PUZZLE SUCCESSFULLY SOLVED. THANK YOU FOR YOUR HELP, MISS FINKLE. YOU HAVE, ONCE AGAIN, ASTONISHED US WITH YOUR ABILITY."

"YOU'RE MOST WELCOME," SHE SAID. "NOW, IF YOU WILL EXCUSE US, MY DEAR FRIEND AND I ARE WELL OVERDUE FOR OUR TEA."

WE BID OUR FAREWELL'S TO DETECTIVE WORTHINGTON AND SERGEANT COLLINS AND, AFTER THE THREE DISTINCT SOUNDS OF HER DOOR UNLOCKING, WE STARTED TO HEAD INSIDE. AS PENNY HAD TAKEN HER FIRST STEP THROUGH THE DOOR, SHE PAUSED AND TURNED BACK TO THE MEN.

"OH, AND SERGEANT COLLINS," SHE SAID. HE TURNED TO LOOK AT HER. "MY BEST OF WISHES FOR YOU AND MISS GARNER. YOU WILL MAKE A WONDERFUL COUPLE."

"THANK YOU, MA'AM," HE SAID, SMILING.

WE PROCEEDED INTO PENNY'S HOUSE WHERE WE ENJOYED OUR OVERDUE POT OF TEA IN THE COMFORT OF MY DEAR FRIEND'S FAMILY ROOM AND WAITED FOR THE NEXT ADVENTURE TO COME OUR WAY.

www.ingramcontent.com/pod-product-compliance
Lightning Source LLC
LaVergne TN
LVHW010437070526
838199LV00066B/6049